Ian's Walk
A Story about Autism

Laurie Lears

ILLUSTRATIONS BY Karen Ritz

Albert Whitman & Company

Morton Grove, Illinois

To Mom and Dad with love. For the Yelnosky family,

and all families challenged by autism. —L. L.

Library of Congress Cataloging-in-Publication Data

Lears, Laurie.

Ian's walk : a story about autism / Laurie Lears ; illustrated by Karen Ritz.

p. cm.

Summary: A young girl realizes how much she cares about her

autistic brother when he gets lost at the park.

ISBN 0-8075-3480-3

[1. Autism—Fiction. 2. Senses and sensation—Fiction.

3. Brothers and sisters—Fiction.] I. Ritz, Karen, ill. II. Title.

PZ7.L46365Ian 1998

[Fic]—dc21   97-27873

CIP AC

A Note about Autism

Siblings of children with disabilities such as autism have extra challenges in their lives. They usually have responsibilities taking care of the brother or sister with autism, whether that sibling is older or younger. They may experience anger that autism has "happened" to their family, embarrassment regarding the way their sibling looks or acts, and feelings of isolation because other children do not have siblings like theirs. As in the case of Julie, the healthy sibling in this book, mixed with these negative feelings are strong feelings of loyalty, responsibility, and love.

Autism is particularly hard to explain to others. Very often the child with autism looks "normal" but reacts so very differently to ordinary situations. The difficulties of understanding autistic disorder and of dealing with the unpredictable behaviors that accompany it make the sibling relationship especially challenging.

It is important that parents acknowledge the negative feelings of brothers and sisters of children with autism. At the same time, parents should stress the strengths of the family and express their appreciation for all the extra things the siblings do. It is essential, too, that parents make sure siblings have time to themselves and time to spend with their own friends.

There are opportunities for personal growth in having a sibling with a disability. The healthy siblings learn valuable lessons of responsibility, compassion, and toleration of differences. They grow to understand that while life is not perfect, it is still good.

Carol P. Rolland, Ph.D.
Chief Psychologist, Developmental Pediatrics
Illinois Masonic Medical Center

Mary Kay McGuire, M.A.
Illinois Masonic Medical Center
Sibling Program Director

It's the perfect day to go to the park and feed the ducks with my big sister, Tara. Except my brother wants to come along, too.

"Aw, Ian, why don't you stay here?" I say. Ian doesn't answer me, though, because he has autism. But he raps his fingers hard against the screen and begins to whine.

"Oh, all right, Ian," I say. "Can he come?" I ask Mom.

"Hmmm…," says Mom. "You'll need to watch him closely the whole time. Are you sure you want to do that?"

"It's okay with me," I answer.

And Tara nods. "You hold his hand, though, Julie," she tells me.

Ian's brain doesn't work like other people's. Ian sees things differently…

When we pass Nan's Diner, Ian steps inside to watch the ceiling fan move in slow circles. He doesn't look at the waitresses hurrying by with all kinds of sandwiches and ice cream.

"Let's get a soda!" I say. But Ian keeps his eyes on the fan until I pull him out the door.

Ian hears things differently...

When a fire truck rushes by with its siren wailing and horn blaring, Ian hardly seems to notice.

But he tilts his head sideways and seems to be listening to something I cannot hear. "Hurry up!" I say, tugging his arm.

Ian smells things differently…

At Mrs. Potter's flower stand, I hold a bouquet of sweet-smelling lilacs up to Ian's face. Ian wrinkles his nose and turns away.

But when we go by the post office, Ian puts his nose against the warm, gritty bricks and sniffs the wall.

"Stop that!" I say. "You look silly!" And I yank him away before anyone notices.

Ian feels things differently…

At the pond, I pick up a soft feather and tickle Ian under his chin. He shrieks and pushes it away.

But while Tara and I toss cereal to the ducks, Ian lies on the ground with his cheek pressed against the hard stones.

"Get up Ian," I say, taking his hand. "Someone might step on you!"

Ian tastes things differently…

When we go past the food booths, Ian won't even look at the pizza, hot dogs, or soft pretzels.

But he reaches into my pocket for the bag of leftover cereal.

"Tara and I don't want to eat cereal for lunch," I tell him. "Come with us while we buy some pizza."

But Ian won't budge. He munches the Power Pops one by one.

Sometimes Ian makes me angry!

"I'll get the pizza," says Tara. "You stay here with Ian, Julie."

I sit down on the bench to wait. "Sit beside me, Ian," I say. But Ian flaps his hands and pays no attention.

At last Tara comes back carrying two slices of gooey pizza.
"Where's Ian?" she asks.

I look at the spot where Ian was standing…but Ian is gone!
My stomach does a flip-flop, and for a moment I can't move.

Tara runs up to a lady. "Have you seen a little boy in a blue shirt?" she cries.

The lady shakes her head. "Perhaps he's watching the baseball game across the park," she suggests.

But Ian does not like baseball.

A man walks by with a little girl on his shoulders. "Have you seen a boy who looks lost?" I say with a lump in my throat.

"No," says the man. "But we're on our way to hear the storyteller. Maybe he's there listening to stories."

But Ian does not like stories.

Tara rushes off to look for Ian. I squeeze my eyes shut and try to think like Ian.

Ian likes the balloon stand where the big machine hisses and stretches balloons into colorful, bobbing shapes.

He likes the water fountain where he can put his face up close and watch the stream of water gush past his eyes.

Suddenly the old bell in the center of the park begins to ring. *Bong, bong, bong!* And then I remember…Ian loves the bell best of all.

I see Tara near the swings, and call to her.
She rushes over, all out of breath, and puts her arms around us.

I run full speed towards the bell. And there's Ian! He is lying under the bell making the big gong move back and forth. I hug him tightly even though he doesn't care for hugs.

"We'll walk home the way *you* like!" I tell Ian.

We stop at the pond and let Ian play with the stones. He lines them up in a straight row along the edge of the walkway. I stand in front of him so no one steps on his fingers.

We walk right past Mrs. Potter's flower stand and stop at the post office instead. Ian sniffs all the bricks he wants, and I don't care who's watching.

When Ian pauses at the corner and seems to be listening to something I cannot hear, we wait patiently, and I try to listen, too.

At Nan's Diner, Ian and I watch the fan until I'm dizzy.

When we finally get home, I say, "It was a good walk, Ian."
And for just a flash, Ian looks at me and smiles.